To Judy, my in-house editor
and the love of my life.

ISBN 978-0997449358

Published by
AMPERSAND, INC.
515 Madison Street
New Orleans, Louisiana 70116

719 Clinton Place
River Forest, Illinois 60305

www.ampersandworks.com

Design
David Robson

Printed in Canada

You'll Know When You See One

ALLAIN C. ANDRY, III Award-winning author of *Louie the Buoy*
Illustrated by KATHLEEN NEWMAN

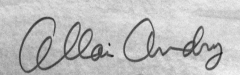

AMP&RSAND, INC.
Chicago • New Orleans

In the Bay of St. Louis, when the tide comes in at night, flounders swim towards the shore and bury themselves in the sand. These fish are flat and round and speckled on top, like giant pancakes with two eyes.

Flounders are so well camouflaged they are difficult to see when buried in the sand. Fishermen carry bright lanterns at night to light the water around them as they look for flounders to spear.

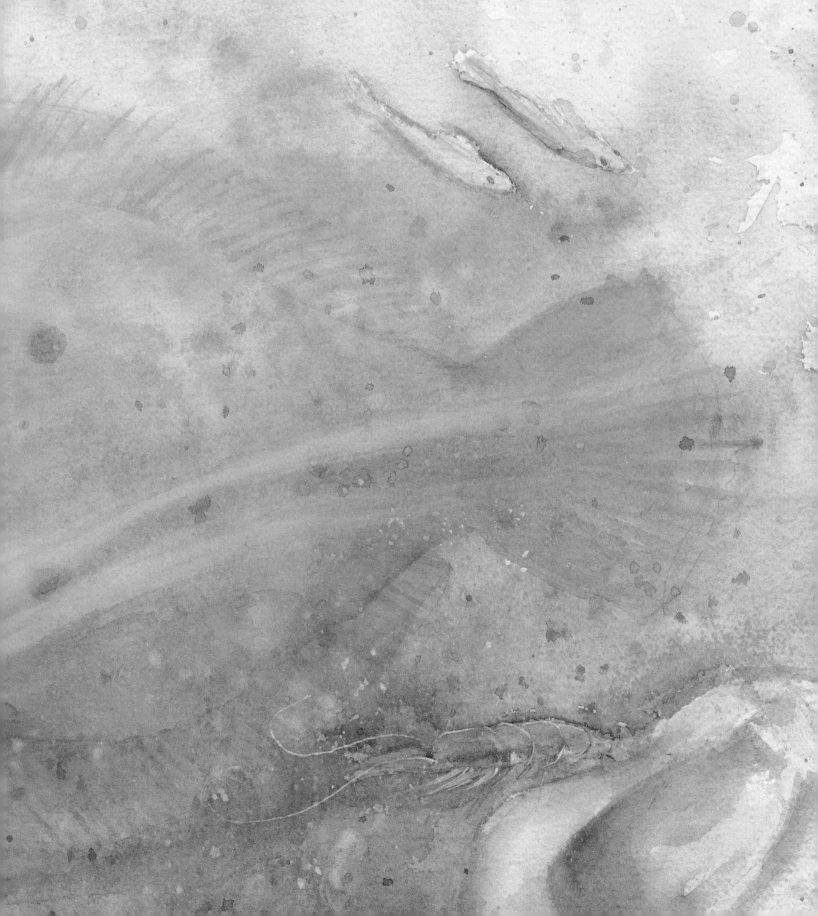

On calm, still nights Katie liked to sit on her pier and watch the lights reflecting in the bay as the fishermen slowly moved back and forth through the shallow water looking for flounders.

When they passed under Katie's pier she would walk quietly in her bare feet looking down through the circle of light to the sandy bottom of the bay. If the fishermen had speared any flounders she would see the fish trailing behind them on a stringer tied to their belts.

Katie had never been floundering herself. She had never seen a live flounder sleeping on the bottom, lightly covered with sand.

Her Dad and brothers, Allain and Michael, went floundering often, especially on nights when the weather was just right.

On those nights Katie and her Mother would build a fire on the beach and wait for the fishermen to return. While hearing about the night's adventures, they had fun eating roasted marshmallows.

One evening after dinner Dad looked at the water, then at his watch. "The wind is still," he said, "there is only a small new moon, so the night is dark and the tide is just starting to move in. It's a fine night for floundering."

The boys were playing kick the can with friends next door. Mother was reading a good book. Dad said, "Kate, let's get some flounders for lunch tomorrow!"

Katie was excited. While Dad went to get the lantern, the spears and the stringer, she quickly put on her old tennis shoes, then ran next door where her brothers were playing.

"How will I know when I see a flounder?" she asked breathlessly. "Oh, it's easy, Katie. You'll know when you see one."

As Dad walked across the lawn the lighted lantern cast long shadows under the pine and oak trees. Katie rushed up to him.

"Dad, how will I know when I see a flounder?"

"Oh, Kate, don't worry, you'll know when you see one."

Together they crossed the dry sand and walked into the shallow water. Katie felt the cool water fill her squishy tennis shoes, and looked slowly around the circle of light made by the lantern.

The bottom of the bay was covered with sandy ridges and small holes like miniature volcanos emitting tiny puffs of sand smoke. She saw crabs scurrying away and shrimp with eyes glowing red in the lantern light. Minnows jumped on the surface of the water and bumped and tickled her legs.

"Look! There's a flounder!" she exclaimed.
"Spear him, Kate!" whispered Dad.

Katie stuck the spear deep into the sand, but when she slowly lifted it out of the water, there was no flounder. She had speared an old shower cap.

They walked on, carefully looking into the water made clear by Dad's circle of light. "I think this is a flounder!"

"Spear him, Kate!" But this time it was an old tennis shoe. On they walked.

"I hope maybe this is a flounder." "Spear him, Kate!"
When the spear made a hard clink, Katie knew this
time it was only a big oyster shell.

Looking for flounders made Katie's eyes play tricks on her. She speared an old sock, a rusted tin can and even a smear of mud with a shell for an eye. "Dad, did you know all those things weren't flounders?"

"Katie, lots of things look like flounders and they can fool you, but when you see a real flounder there will be no doubt in your mind. You'll know when you see one."

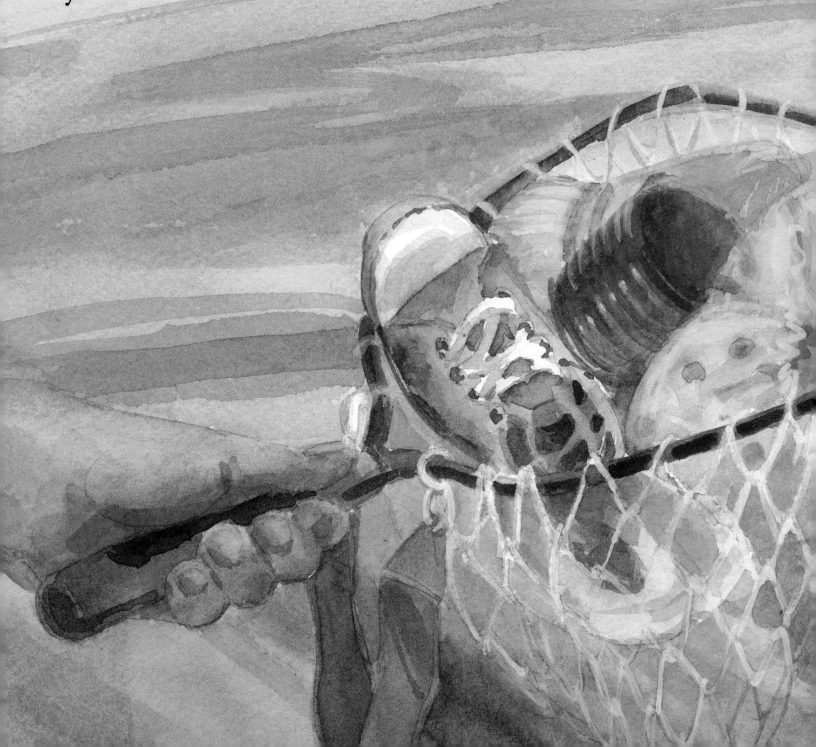

Between the pilings of the pier something caught Katie's eye. She knew this was a flounder. Even though it was lightly covered with sand, she could clearly see the outline of the its flat speckled body, its tail and its two eyes. Katie moved slowly and held the spear right above the sleeping fish.

"Spear him, Kate!" Katie didn't move. She no longer wanted to spear it. "Dad, I learned something from this flounder tonight. You really do know when you see one. Maybe I will let him go now and catch him with my fishing pole tomorrow."

"Well then, just touch the side of its tail with the edge of your spear and see what happens." Katie gently nudged her spear down beside the flounder's tail.

As the flounder exploded from its bed, Katie was so surprised she almost dropped her spear. She and Dad laughed. All she could see were puffs of sand where its tail hit the bottom in its rush for deep water and safety.

Katie and her Dad slowly walked home through the water then took off their squishy tennis shoes. Her brothers had started building a fire and Mother came down with a bag of marshmallows.

They all sat on the warm sand, watching the other floundering lights moving back and forth along the shallow shore of the bay.

With a confident smile on her face Katie turned to her brothers and said, "You and Dad were right. You really do know when you see one!"

What Is It That Katie Is Hoping to Spear?
(*A Natural History of the Southern Flounder*)

Flounders belong to the family of flat fish, which include European Place, Turbot, Sole, and the huge Atlantic and Pacific Halibut, which can weigh up to 400 pounds. The most common flounder on the Mississippi Gulf Coast is the Southern Flounder, which generally lives in shallow saline estuaries such as the Bay of St. Louis. These are mainly female flounders which are about 24 inches in length, on average. Male founders are much smaller, averaging only 10 to 14 inches. The males stay in deeper water where they are joined by the females in November and December for spawning.

Southern Flounders spawn for approximately two months. During this time each female releases several hundred thousand fertilized eggs which turn into larvae in two to three days and drift on the water's surface feeding on plankton. These larvae resemble most fish, with one eye on each side of their heads, and they swim upright moving their tails from side to side. They are carried by tides into shallow bays and estuaries.

After approximately 50 days an incredible change occurs. The flounder's right eye slowly moves to the left side of its body near the left eye. Its left, or upper side, turns dark while the right, or lower side, becomes white. Flounders move by making an up and down motion with its body and tail. Most fish swim by moving their bodies from side to side.

Since the flounder is flat, it can lie on the sandy bottom and is able to change the color and patterning of its skin to match its surroundings. It uses its fins to lightly cover itself with a small amount of sand, which makes it almost invisible to its prey. Flounders generally dine on shrimp and small fish.

Flounders are prized as tasty seafood whether fried, baked or sautéed. A broiled flounder stuffed with fresh crabmeat is a gourmet delight on the Gulf Coast. I hope each of you will enjoy catching and eating a flounder. You will find more detailed information on the website of the Southern Mississippi Gulf Coast Research Laboratory entitled Southern and Gulf Coast Flounders, which also includes beautiful drawings and photographs. http://gcrl.usm.edu/public/fish/flounder.php

—*Allain C. Andry, III*

About the Author and Illustrator

Allain C. Andry, III is an attorney and former banking executive in New Orleans. He and his wife, Judy, live in the French Quarter and summer in Asheville, North Carolina. They spent as much time as possible for fifty years with their children and grandchildren at their home on the Bay of St. Louis in Pass Christian, Mississippi, before it was destroyed by Hurricane Katrina. He is a humorous and gifted storyteller whose stories have entertained family and friends for generations. The photo above was taken in 1986.

Kathleen Newman began playing with art supplies at a very early age and went on to study at the American Academy of Art and the Art Institute in Chicago. She now wins awards for her pastel, oil and watercolor paintings and teaches weekly classes at the Old Town Art Center in Chicago as well as painting workshops throughout the United States. She and her husband live in Chicago and compete in the annual Race to Mackinac each summer on their J105 with their two children and family crew. **www.kathleennewman.com**

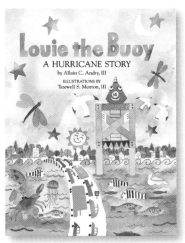

Andry is also the author of *LOUIE THE BUOY: A Hurricane Story*, the first of his trilogy of stories set on the Gulf Coast of Mississippi. *LOUIE THE BUOY* won the 2009 Writers Digest International Gold Medal Award for the best Children's Picture Book. Tazewell S. Morton, III, who illustrated *LOUIE*, is also the only artist in the world to have a flag that he designed planted on the moon. The Louisiana Philharmonic Orchestra commissioned a score for *LOUIE THE BUOY*, which premiered on February 21, 2016 in New Orleans. A professional actress read the text and illustrations from the book were projected onto a huge screen while the orchestra performed for a full house of enthusiastic fans.